AN ANCIENT AFRICAN VILLAGE TRICK

VIVIAN VAN GORDER

ISBN: 978-1-63950-194-6 (sc)
ISBN: 978-1-63950-195-3 (e)

Writers Apex

Gateway Towards Success

8063 MADISON AVE #1252
Indianapolis, IN 46227
+13176596889
www.writersapex.com

nce upon a time long, long ago, and far, far away—in a lovely, little village called Ibusa, in West Africa - there lived a sweet little, boy named Santo.

Santo was a strong boy, six-years old with a three-year old sister, Ashanti. The two of them played together hour after hour in their lovely, little village, where everyone knows everyone, and loves everyone, and watches out for each other. Everyone plays together, and eats together, and cries together, and cares for each other with thoughtfulness.

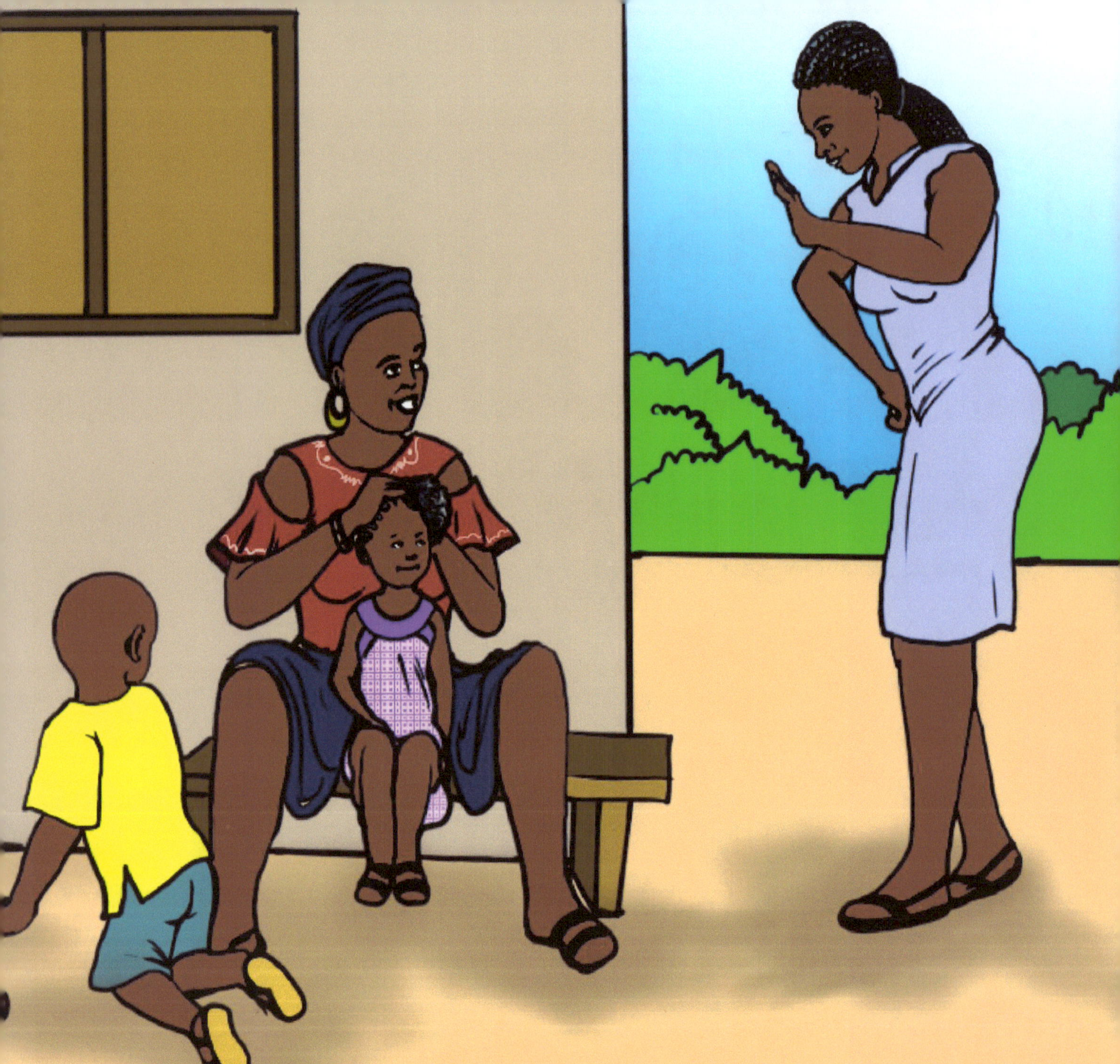

One day, Santo was playing at home and Mum was braiding Ashanti's hair, when Auntie Carol came walking by their house.

"Good afternoon!" said Auntie Carol.

"Ahhh, Are you going to the market?" Mum asked Auntie Carol.

"Indeed I am!" Auntie Carol replied. "And how are you doing today, lovely little Santo?"

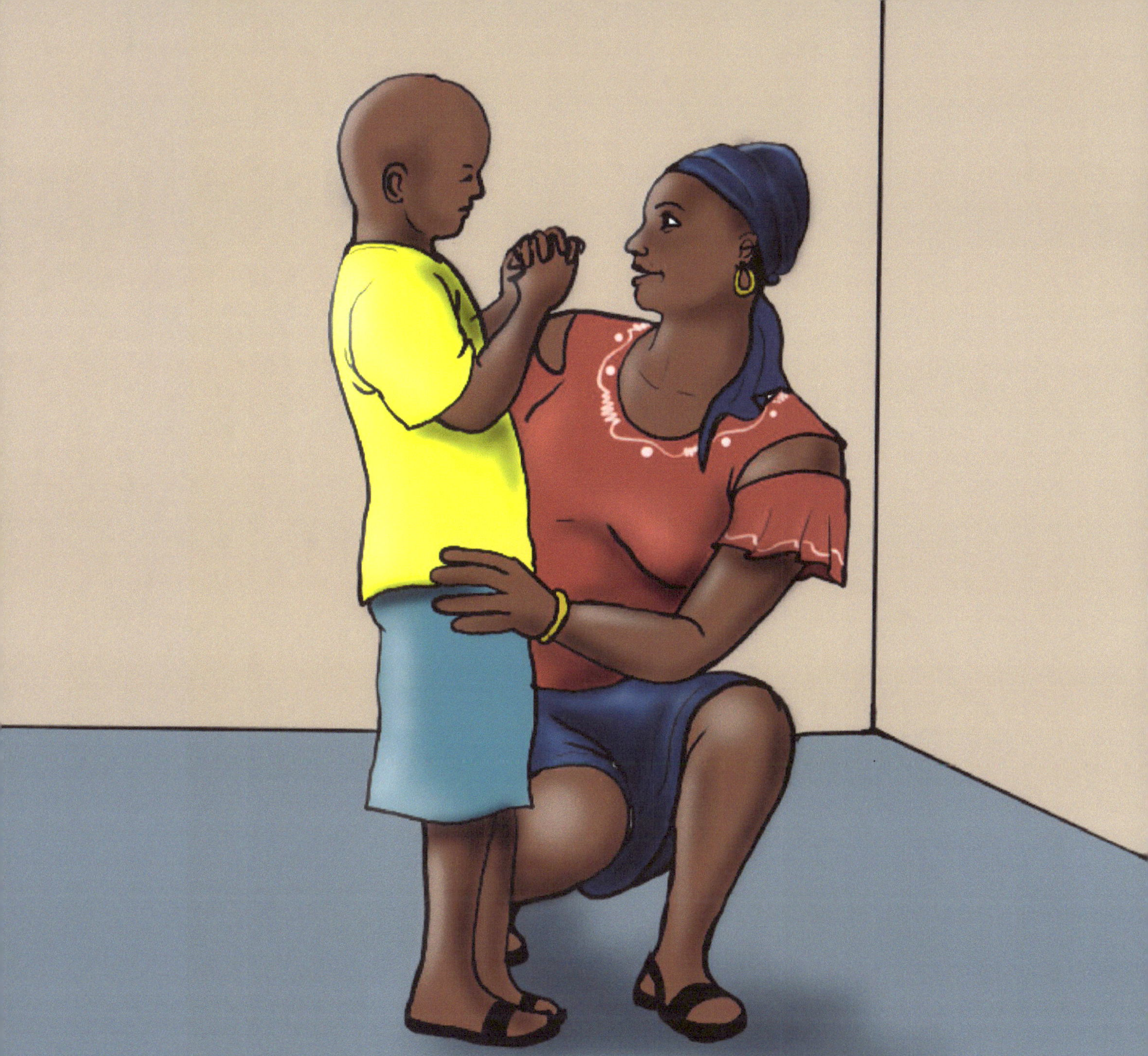

Santo answered, "I am doing fine, Miss Carol!" Mum corrected Santo: "My lovely little boy, how many times have I told you to call Miss Carol, 'Auntie Carol?'"

"Mamma," Santo asked, "Why do we call every woman, 'Auntie', and every man in our village, 'Uncle?'"

"My lovely little boy!" Mum replied, "Listen to me: Every elder in our village is, 'Auntie' or 'Uncle,' because this is how we show loving respect for our elders in Africa."

"I promise I will do better next time," Santo said. Soon after, it was time for dinner. Mamma set down a plate of yam porridge in front of little Santo. As soon as the porridge was in front of him, Santo quickly began to gobble it down without taking a breath.

Mamma corrected Santo, "My lovely, little boy! Listen to me: Slowly eat your food because this is how we show loving respect to our parents, for our food, in Africa."

"I promise I will do better next time," Santo said.

In Africa, after everyone else is served, the mum eats her food in peace. One afternoon, Santo interrupted his mum while she was trying to eat her meal, and so his mum said to him: "Please, little Santo go for me, to Auntie Ama's house and tell her that I am sending you to her to bring back home, ''Omu Nwa Ri.''

"Mum! What is 'Omu Nwa Ri?'" asked little Santo.

"Go! Little boy, Auntie knows what it is!" mum replied.

As Santo was going towards Auntie Ama's, he saw his friend Kambu playing with the other children. Kambu invited Santo to join them, but Santo explained that he was running an errand for his mum.

When Santo reached Auntie Ama's house at the far end of Ibusa village, he asked her for "Omu Nwa Ri."

"Ahhh!" said Auntie Ama, with a knowing smile on her face. "I just gave 'Omu Nwa Ri' to Auntie Tomato. Go to her house and she will help you on your errand."

On his way to Auntie Tomato's house, he saw his friend Sandy, dancing in colorful costumes in a circle with the other children of Ibusa. "Come dance! It's the Iwu Festival!"

However, Santo explained that he was running an errand for his mum. He left Sandy and friends, on his way to Auntie Tomato's house.

When Santo met Auntie Tomato, he explained that his mum had sent him to collect "Omu Nwa Ri" from her. "Ahhh!" said Auntie Tomato, with a knowing smile on her face. "I just gave 'Omu Nwa Ri' to Auntie Shakara. Go to her house, and she will help you on your errand."

While Santo's was heading to Auntie Shakara's house, at the far end of Ibusa village, he saw a lady lifting a tray of mangoes onto her head, and before he knew it, he saw money fall from her pocket to the ground, without her realizing she had lost it.

Santo picked up the money and ran towards the lady.

"Excuse me!" Santo shouted. The lady stopped—assuming Santo wanted to buy some mangoes, but Santo handed her the money and explained that she had accidentally dropped it on the ground. The lady quickly checked her pockets and discovered her money was gone.

She was so happy that she offered to give Santo some mangoes but he refused, "No, Auntie! I was just doing the right thing, bringing back to you what belongs to you."

The woman was so happy that she said, "You are such a good little boy, Santo, and I am sure your mummy is so proud of you!" And so, he continued on his errand.

When Santo met Auntie Shakara, he explained that his mum had sent him to collect, ''Omu Nwa Ri,'' from her. "I went to Auntie Ama's, and she sent me to Auntie Tomato's, and she sent me to you. Please help me! I am so tired—running all over Ibusa village asking for 'Omu Nwa Ri.'" "Ahh!" said Auntie Shakara, with a knowing smile on her face. "I just gave 'Omu Nwa Ri' to Auntie Okazi only 5 minutes ago. I know you are frustrated; please take some roasted corn for your journey, and also take some to your mum."

''Thank you Auntie !'' Santo exclaimed.

And he continued on his errand.

As Santo approached Auntie Okazi's house, he saw his friend Blah-blah, waiting at her door. "What are you doing here, Blah-blah?" Santo asked.

"I am here on an errand for my mum who asked me to collect, 'Omu Nwa Ri', from Auntie Okazi, but I do not know what it is''.

"Hmmm!" Santo exclaimed. "Something is fishy here! My mum also sent me to collect, 'Omu Nwa Ri', and I also do not know what it is."

Just then, their friend, Ada, also arrived at Auntie Okazi's door. Both Santo and Blah-Blah asked Ada, at the same time, "Did your mum send you here to collect 'Omu Nwa Ri'?"

"How did you know?" asked Ada. The three friends compared their stories and knew something was up. All of them had been given the run-around by the mums of Ibusa village. It was time to solve the mystery. They would ask Wise Elder Mazi to explain 'Omu Nwa Ri.' And so all three of them continued on their errand.

Wise Elder Mazi was the oldest, wisest man in Ibusa village. When Elder Mazi asked the children why they had come to visit, Santo asked, "Wise Elder Mazi, explain 'Omu Nwa Ri'—Our mothers asked us to bring 'Omu Nwa Ri', but none of us know what it is!"

Elder Mazi laughed. "Ha! ha ha! 'Omu Nwa Ri', is the most ancient trick in all Ibusa!" At this, all of the children exclaimed with surprise, "The village trick?" they echoed.

Elder Mazi said, "Sit down, little children, let me tell you a story: Long, long ago, a woman in our village, called Mama Sara, had a son who bothered her whenever she was trying to eat her food peacefully. She asked him to stop, but he never listened. This went on every day. Finally, Mama Sara went to Mama Marble, the wisest woman in the village, and Mama Marble told her about, 'Omu Nwa Ri', which had worked for all of the mother's in the Ibusa village whenever their children bothered them when trying to eat their meals peacefully."

''Mums would send a child from house to house, asking them to bring 'Omu Nwa Ri', which tells everyone that the child has been bothering his/her mum, who needs some peace. This is when they send the child to another house until mama has had time to finish her food in peace. Only then, will the child be sent home.''

"Wow!" said all of the three village children at once. "Thank you Wise Elder Mazi! From now on, we will not bother our mamas when they are eating their meals."

Santo went home and found his mum working. "Mum! Mum! I now understand the meaning of you asking me to collect 'Omu Nwa Ri.' I promise I will leave you in peace and never bother you whenever you are eating, It was selfish of me for not thinking about you; Mum! I promise I will do better next time," Santo said with joy.

Mum hugged Santo. "I knew you were a smart little boy. I am so proud of you! Now, you know the mums' playful trick of Ibusa village."

Then, both Mum and Santo laughed and smiled as they hugged and hugged.

THE END.